DOES A DUCK HAVE A DADDY?

Fred Ehrlich, M.D.
Pictures by **Emily Bolam**

 Blue Apple Books
Maplewood, N.J.

For William and Nathaniel

Text copyright © 2004 by Fred Ehrlich
Illustrations copyright © 2004 by Emily Bolam

CIP Data is available.
First published in the United States 2004 by
🍎 Blue Apple Books
P.O. Box 1380, Maplewood, N.J. 07040
www.blueapplebooks.com
First published in paperback by Blue Apple Books 2007
Distributed in the U.S. by Chronicle Books

First Paperback Edition
Printed in China

ISBN 13: 978-1-59354-590-1
ISBN 10: 1-59354-590-8

1 3 5 7 9 10 8 6 4 2

Does a butterfly have a daddy?
Does a bug?

All animal babies begin life because of a male and a female parent. Some babies—such as snakes and insects—can crawl or fly away as soon as they hatch.

They don't need parents to take care of them, so the mother and the father leave after the eggs are laid.

Does a fish have a daddy?

Fish are also animals that can swim away as soon
as they hatch. A baby fish never knows which
big fish is its mother or its father.

Does a duck have a daddy?

A baby duck can recognize its mother but not
its father. A duckling will follow the first thing
it *sees* after it comes out of the egg—
and that is usually its mother.

Some animal fathers work very hard
to take care of their babies.

A father blue jay helps the mother feed the helpless baby birds juicy insects and worms... until the babies can fly and find food on their own.

After a female emperor penguin lays an egg, the father takes care of the egg.

While the mother swims out to sea to fatten herself up with food, the male penguin keeps the egg on top of its feet. The warm skin and feathers on his belly cover the egg like a blanket and protect it from the icy cold.

When the baby penguin hatches, its mother
comes back from the sea, healthy and fat,
so she can feed her baby.

The male sea horse is an unusual father. Instead of the mother, it's the dad that gives birth!

The mother lays her eggs in a special pouch in the father's stomach. The eggs hatch inside the pouch, and the baby sea horses stay there until they grow strong.

When they are big enough to take care of themselves, the babies leave the pouch and swim away.

Every year a female beaver has four or five babies.

Beaver babies can swim soon after they are born, but they are not ready to be on their own. The parents feed and protect their young for many months.

Baby beavers stay with their parents for two years, then go off to mate and start their own families.

Baboons are primates, the group of mammals that includes monkeys, apes, and people. When primate babies are born, they can't do anything for themselves.

This daddy baboon baby-sits while the mommy looks for food. He carries the baby and protects it from enemies.

Baboons, monkeys, and apes all spend a long time with their parents—two to three years— before they venture out on their own.

But no animal spends as long
in its parents' care as a child.

A human baby has the longest childhood of any animal.

Human daddies are unique. They spend more time with their children than any other animal father.

They carry them, play with them,
feed them, protect them, and teach them.

Children learn all of these things, and more, from their mommies and daddies:

to talk

to keep
themselves clean

to stay safe

to have good manners

to get along
with others

to read and write

Human daddies are special.
Isn´t yours?

Garfield
BELLY LAUGHS

BY JIM DAVIS

Ballantine Books • New York

A Ballantine Books Trade Paperback Original

Copyright © 2019 by PAWS, Inc. All Rights Reserved.
"GARFIELD" and the GARFIELD characters are trademarks of PAWS, Inc.
Based on the Garfield® characters created by Jim Davis.

Published in the United States by Ballantine Books, an imprint of Random House,
a division of Penguin Random House LLC, New York.

BALLANTINE and the HOUSE colophon are registered trademarks of Penguin Random House LLC.

NICKELODEON is a Trademark of Viacom International, Inc.

All of the comics in this work have been previously published.

ISBN 978-1-9848-1777-8
Ebook ISBN 978-1-9848-1778-5

Printed in China on acid-free paper

randomhousebooks.com

9 8 7 6 5 4 3

Hudson Area Public Library
PO Box 461
Hudson, IL 61748

JIM DAVIS 7-30

SOME DAYS, YOU JUST GOTTA DANCE

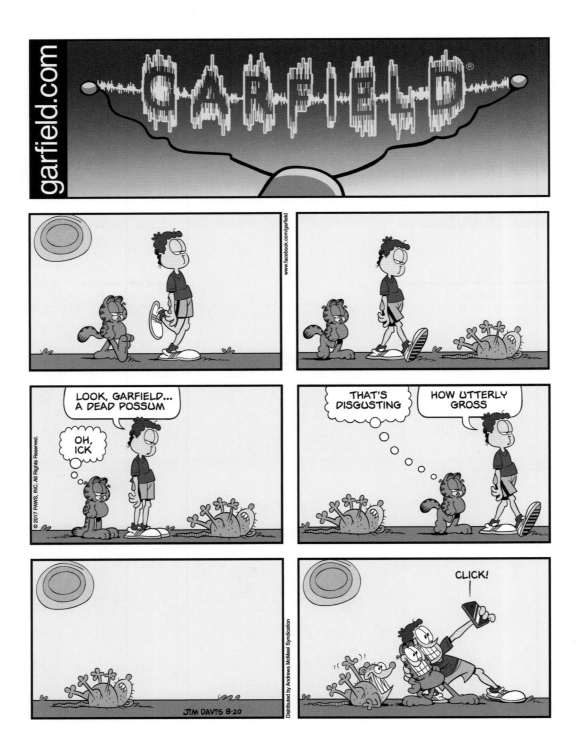

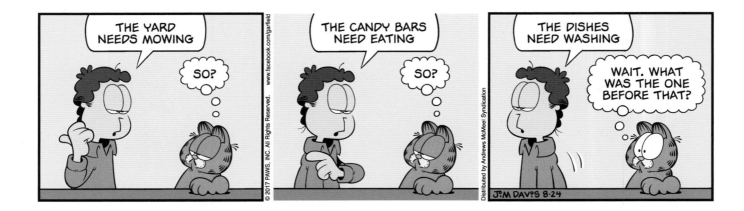

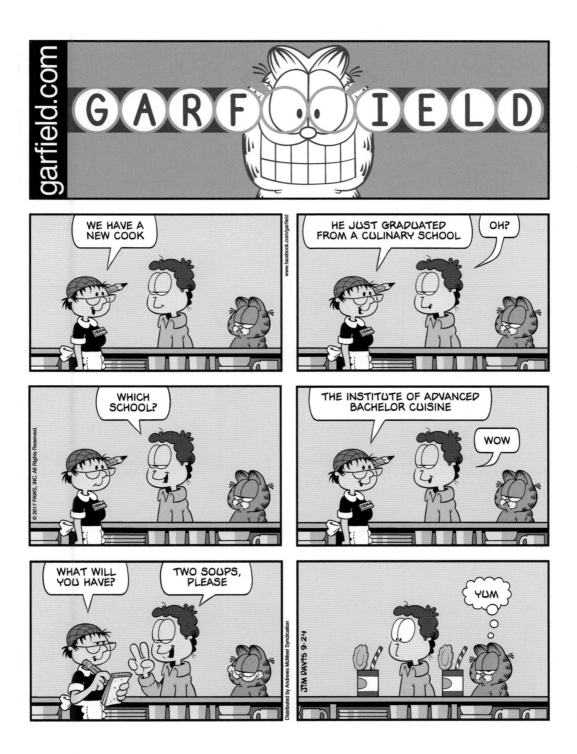

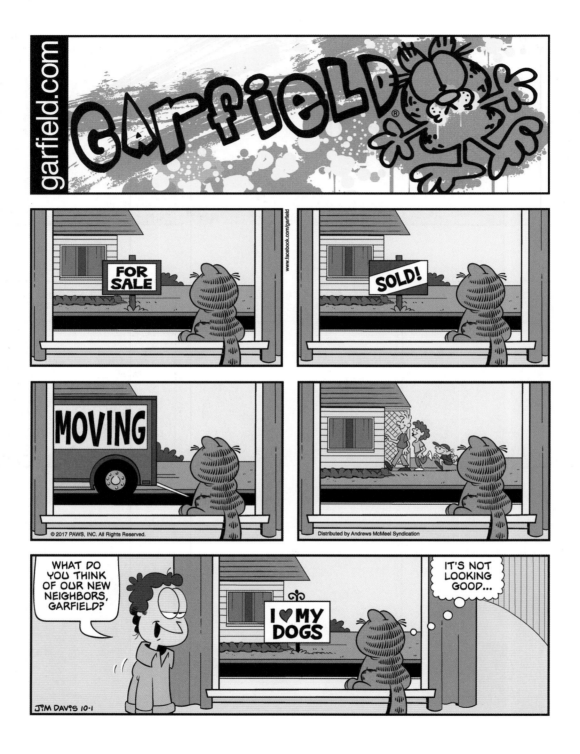

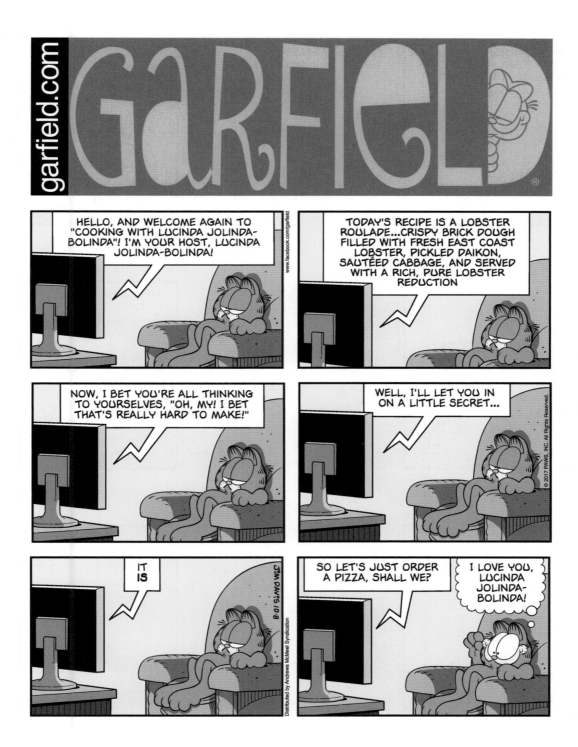

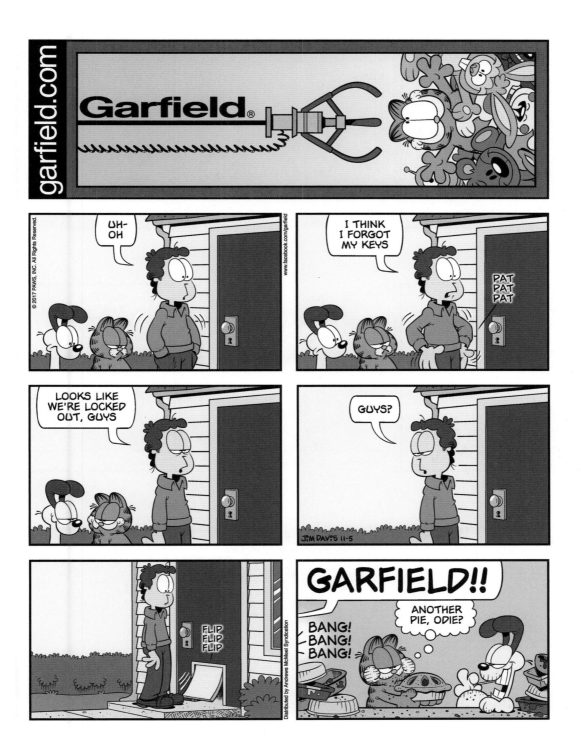

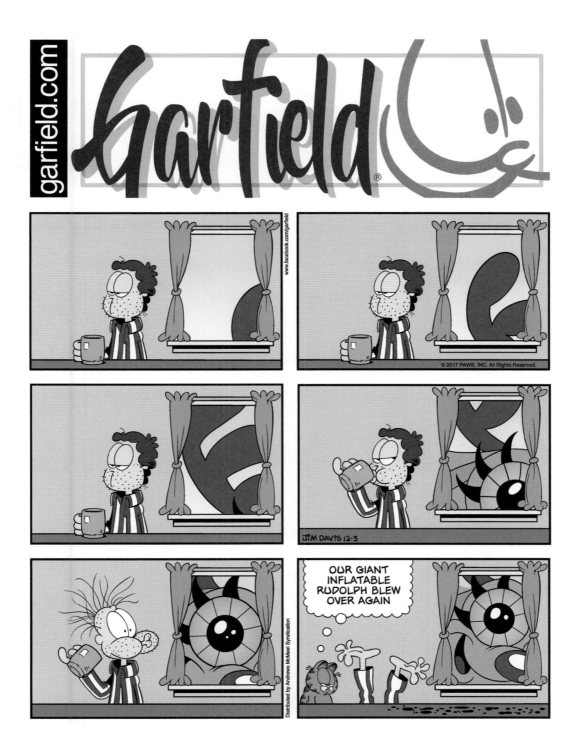

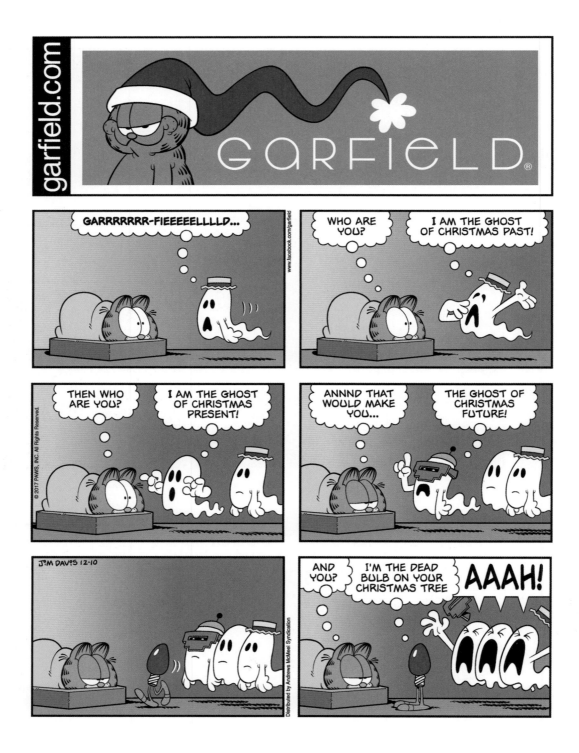

ONE WEEK TO CHRISTMAS, POOKY! CAN YOU STAND THE EXCITEMENT?!

DON'T BE FOOLED. UNDER THAT CALM EXTERIOR, HE'S A QUIVERING MESS

I WONDER WHAT ODIE WOULD LIKE FOR CHRISTMAS

HE WASN'T SURE

SO I TOLD HIM HE MIGHT FIND SOME IDEAS ONLINE

STINKY, SMELLY THINGS

YOU HAVEN'T LIVED UNTIL YOU'VE TRIED HIS HOMEMADE MOUSENOG

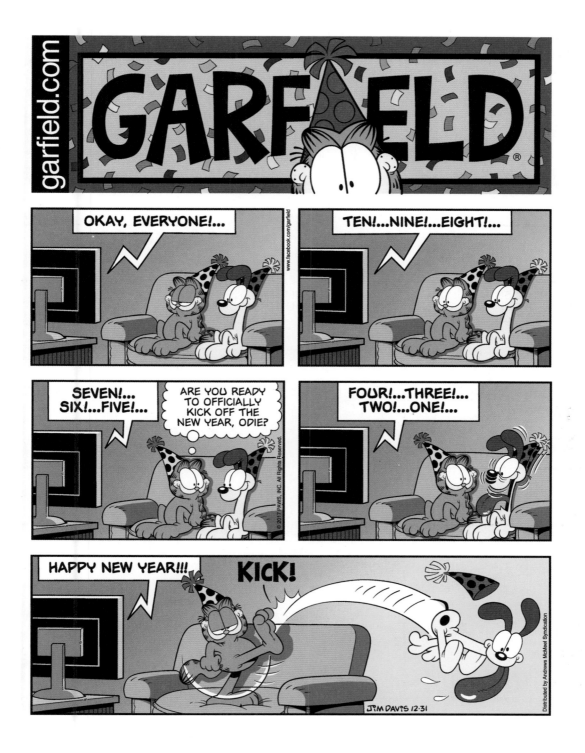

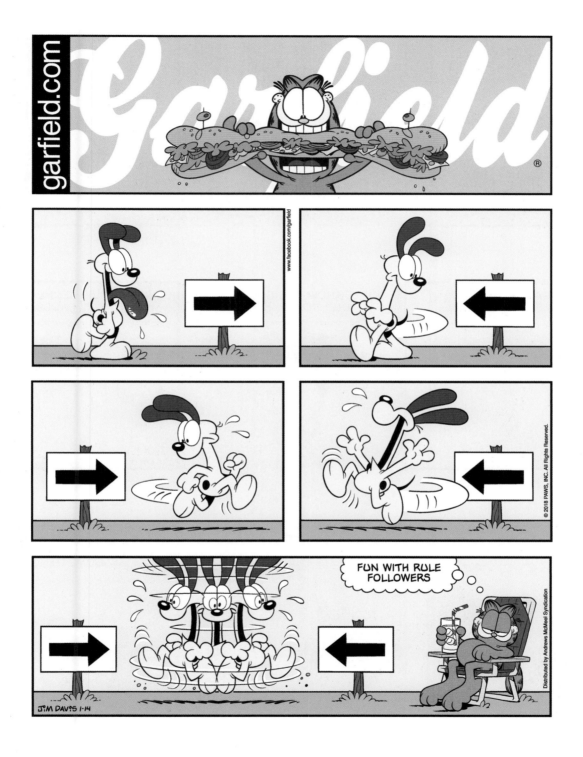

FUN WITH RULE
FOLLOWERS

JIM DAVIS 1-14

91